AQUAMARINE

AQUAMARINE

ALICE HOFFMAN

APPLE SIGNATURE

SCHOLASTIC INC.

New York   Toronto   London   Auckland   Sydney
Mexico City   New Delhi   Hong Kong   Buenos Aires

No part of this publication may be
reproduced, stored in a retrieval
system, or transmitted in any form
or by any means, electronic, mech-
anical, photocopying, recording, or
otherwise, without written
permission of the publisher.
For information regarding
permission, write to Scholastic
Inc., Attention: Permissions
Department, 557 Broadway,
New York, NY 10012.

ISBN-13: 978-0-439-09864-9
ISBN-10: 0-439-09864-5

23 24 25 26 27   12 13 14 15/0

Printed in the U.S.A. 23
First Scholastic paperback
edition, September 2001

Original hardcover edition
designed by Elizabeth Parisi,
published by Scholastic
Press, April 2001

The text type was set in
Adobe Garamond. Display type was
set in Gunther Pen.
Watercolors by
Goro Sasaki.

To Carol and Allison DeKnight

and to Jo Ann,

who believed in mermaids

—A.H.

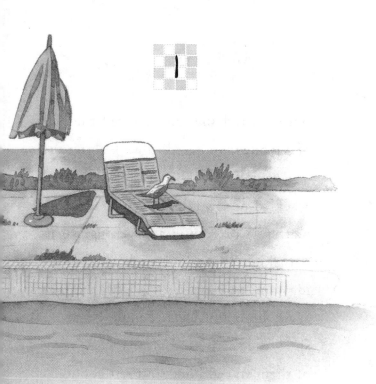

AT THE CAPRI BEACH CLUB, every
day was hotter and hotter until the
asphalt in the parking lot began to
bubble. Snow cones and ice-cream
sandwiches melted as soon as they
were removed from the snack shop's

freezers, and the sand burned the feet of anyone who dared to walk along the beach at noon. The heat popped and crackled and wouldn't let up. It didn't matter if there was an evening storm with high winds and buckets of pouring rain; by morning the sky was once again blue and clear. People began to sit in the shade, and after a while most of them stayed home in their cool, air-conditioned rooms. Even those families who had been coming to the beach club for years gave up their memberships and found other ways to while away the scorching days of August.

The Capri had been more run-down

every season, but this year was clearly the worst. No wonder the owner was closing the club at the end of the month. Weeds were sprouting in the tennis courts, beach umbrellas were filled with holes, seagulls had taken over the pool area, nesting on chaise lounges and sipping chlorinated water. The lifeguards had gone out on strike in July, and had never returned. Even the cafeteria had closed down — the windows were boarded over, the door nailed shut — leaving only the snack shop, run by Raymond, who would soon be going off to college in Miami and was far too busy reading to fix a sandwich or fetch a glass of lemonade.

The only people who still came to the Capri every day were two twelve-year-old girls and they didn't mind the heat one bit. Hailey and Claire had lived next door to each other and been best friends all their lives. Unlike most people in town, they wanted this summer to go on forever, no matter how humid or hot. They both hoped that August would continue beyond the confines of its thirty-one days, in a blaze of sunshine and heat. These girls had stopped looking at calendars. They didn't wear watches. They shut their eyes when the first star appeared in the sky. The reason they wished every day to be the same was that at the end of the month, Claire would be moving to Florida with her grandparents and Hailey would be left behind.

"Don't talk about it," Hailey said whenever Claire brought up the subject. "Don't even think about it."

For although Hailey thought nothing of leaping from the highest diving platform or swimming so far out to sea that she disappeared from sight, she was easily frightened by other things — a future she couldn't control, for instance, or the notion that a lifelong friendship might be lost at the end of the week when the Capri closed down for good and Claire moved away.

As for Claire, she was quiet and shy and as afraid of water as Hailey was drawn to it. She had lost both her parents in an accident on the expressway, and ever since, her vision of the world had darkened. She'd become skittish, forsaking those things which brought other girls joy. Swimming, for instance, made her so nervous she refused to dip her toes into shallow water, not even on a burning hot day.

Between the two friends, Claire had

always been the problem solver. She was the sort of girl who could take an old dress, stitch a hem, add a sash, and wind up with an outfit that made it seem as though she'd just walked out of the finest store. Given a patch of bare ground and some flower seeds, she would soon have the prettiest garden on the block. But now Claire was faced with a problem she couldn't solve.

She had begged and she'd pleaded, promising to never again ask for another favor if only they could stay, but her grandparents had already sold their house and rented an apartment in Florida, right on the beach. As if an oceanfront view mattered to Claire. As if she ever wanted to go to any beach but the one at the Capri where she and Hailey had spent every summer of their lives.

Both girls knew that things changed, sometimes for the worse. Claire had lost her parents and Hailey's mother and father had been divorced, and now her mother worked long hours and hadn't any time to have fun. But the Capri had always stayed the same, a place to hold on to even in the darkest days of winter when snow piled up by their back doors.

All summer long, the girls had been

dropped off at the Capri by Hailey's mom on her way to work, and picked up at six o'clock sharp by Claire's grandfather, Maury. Maury was so happy to be moving to Florida that all the neighbors agreed he now looked at least ten years younger, much better than he had last winter when he'd broken his leg after slipping on a patch of slick ice. He'd needed to use a wheelchair until the following spring, and it was this accident which had convinced Claire's grandmother it was time to relocate to a place where winter was no longer a concern for what she called rickety old bones.

"What's new, Susie Q's?" Maury

would always say when the two friends traipsed through the heat waves that rose up in the parking lot at the end of the day. Time was speeding forward regardless of their wishes. No matter how slowly they dragged their feet, every day was still twenty-four hours closer to moving day.

Whenever they left the Capri, they'd see Raymond's motorbike parked in the shadows of the breezeway. But there wasn't another vehicle in sight. Who would want to spend their precious summer days at a beach club that had become a disaster area? Beyond a wire fence, several bulldozers were al-

ready at work tearing down the play-
ground where the swings had long ago
rusted into place. Still, it hadn't been
that many summers since Hailey and
Claire had ridden those swings into the
sky, up through the heat waves and the
white clouds, convinced they had all
the time in the world.

Now, in the last days of the Capri,
time seemed to be their enemy. Sometimes, when they looked into the mirror in the changing room of the cabana,
where bathing suits and towels were
stored, they didn't even look like themselves anymore. Their legs were too
long, their arms too rangy, their hair

cut too short to be pulled into pony-tails or braids.

Each day when Claire's grandfather asked "What's new, Susie Q's?" the girls always responded, "Nothing" in voices so glum, anyone would think they had no hope whatsoever for what the future might bring. By next summer, the Capri would be a bird sanctuary, and although the girls were happy for the birds, they didn't understand why this one piece of their lives couldn't go on as before.

Once the bulldozers started in on the wooden cabanas, once they destroyed the pool and the patio and the snack bar, wasn't it possible that Claire would no longer remember summers spent at the Capri with her parents? Would Hailey still recall how her father took her swimming in the farthest waves when her mom and dad were still married? When the Capri was gone, maybe they would forget each other as well. They'd grow up and be just like all those other people who didn't know what it meant to have your best friend living right next door, grown-ups who had no idea of what it was like to have someone understand you so well they could tell what you were thinking even before you spoke aloud.

■ ▫ ■

The last days of August were identical, blistering mornings fading into white-hot afternoons. At the start of the day, the girls sat by the pool, trailing their fingers in the water and shooing the seagulls away. At lunch time, they bothered Raymond, who seemed much too handsome to be as nice as he was. He never minded when Hailey and Claire sat at the counter for hours, drinking lemonade and watching him read. In past summers, there had been flocks of teenaged girls hanging around Raymond, but all those girls' families had joined town pools or rented summer houses, and only Hailey and Claire remained to admire him. Late in the afternoon, when it was almost time to go, the girls walked along the beach. Sometimes Hailey went in for a swim to cool off, but Claire stayed on the shore, adding to her collection of stones and shells.

And so every day blended into the next, until one morning there was a storm with gusts of sixty miles an hour and extraordinarily high tides. The girls had to stay home that day, and they shivered at the nearness of September. They barely said a word all afternoon. That night, in houses right next door to each other, neither one could sleep. The wind was so strong, it knocked on the rooftops and rattled the stars up above. Both Hailey and Claire had the feeling that something was about to happen, in spite of how much they wanted their lives to remain the same.

■ ■ ■

When they arrived at the beach club the next morning, they found that the storm had left its mark. The wooden paths were littered with purple snails.

Starfish and scallops were trapped in the fountain at the center of the patio and the snack bar was missing its roof. The pool had been roped off and a NO SWIMMING sign had been hastily installed by the owner, who hardly even bothered to visit the club anymore.

The water in the pool was as thick as soup. Seaweed clogged up the filter. Barnacles clung to the blue-and-white tiles and luminous moon jellyfish slowly drifted by. Hailey, who had learned how to swim in this very pool when she was only a toddler, was outraged at what a mess it had become.

"What difference does it make?"

Claire said. "After next Saturday, they'll drain the pool and bulldoze it, too."

Even though she had never dared swim in the pool, there were tears in Claire's eyes as she gazed into the murky waters. For the first time in a long while, she had no idea of what to do next. Maybe that was why Hailey ducked under the ropes to take a closer look.

Hailey had always been fearless and a little too curious for her own good, but she'd always had Claire there behind her, urging her on, concocting their plans. She stuck her toes in the water and wondered what would become of

her once she was all by herself. A no-
body, a nothing, with no one to talk to
and no one to call in the middle of the
night when she heard her mother crying, or when a stray dog knocked over
a garbage can. Hailey stood at the very
edge of the pool. Before Claire could
tell her it wasn't a good idea, before she
lost all of her courage, she dove in.

Hailey was such a good diver, there
wasn't a sound when she entered the
water, just a series of ripples circling
out from the center of the pool. Claire
quickly clambered over the ropes and
ran to the spot where Hailey had last
been standing, making certain to hold

onto the railing so she wouldn't fall in herself. Claire had spent her whole life worrying that her friend would do something foolish and jump in headfirst where she didn't belong, and now Hailey had done exactly that.

The strange, cloudy water made Claire more nervous about the pool than she usually was. She had never even learned the Dead Man's Float, which, when you really thought about it, wasn't the most comforting name. You never could tell what might happen in the water. You'd have to have faith in yourself to dive in, and that was something Claire didn't possess.

Sixty seconds later, Hailey came bursting back through the surface, sputtering and shaking with cold. She dragged herself up the rungs of the ladder, too chilled and breathless to speak. In the deep end of the pool, the moon jellyfish rode the current through strands of brown seaweed.

Best friends don't need to be told when something extraordinary has happened, and this was the case with Hailey and Claire. One look, and Claire knew that her friend's swim had been anything but ordinary.

"What did you see?" Claire asked. "What's down there?"

Hailey didn't say, *You'll never believe me,* which is what she would have told anyone else. She knew Claire would believe her, no matter what, so she whispered the name of what she'd seen in the deep end of the pool where everything was hazy and dim. Claire held even more tightly to the railing, lest she fall in and be faced with the creature Hailey had seen, because she absolutely, positively, without a doubt, believed.

On this day when Claire's grandfather asked, "What's new Susie Q's?" the girls stared at each other, eyes shining.

"Nothing," they said together, the way best friends often do. Of course, what they really meant was that they weren't quite sure. What they meant was that for the first time in a very long while, they couldn't wait for morning to come.

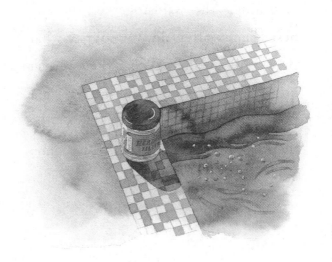

THE NEXT DAY, as soon as they got out
of Hailey's mother's car in the parking
lot, Hailey was the one who took
charge. After all, she'd been the one to
see the mermaid at the bottom of the
pool, huddled in a murky corner, her

long hair streaming. Claire wouldn't have ventured into the water for any reason, not even to see such a wondrous being.

As they went through the entrance-way to the Capri, Hailey handed her friend a jar she'd stored in her backpack. Claire held the jar up to the light and tried her best to figure out what the slippery-looking things were inside.

"Herring," Hailey told her when Claire couldn't venture a guess. "It's a kind of marinated fish. I found it in the back of the pantry. Mermaids must get hungry. All we need to do is hide behind the diving board, and when she comes to the surface to eat, we can study her."

"Good plan," Claire said. At any other time, Claire would have been the one to come up with the plans, but lately she'd been up half the night, thinking about how her sweaters and boots would be pointless in Florida, and how the leaves wouldn't change in the fall, and how it would be summer all year long.

Hailey, herself, was somewhat surprised to find that she'd actually been the one with the ideas. "You really think it's a good plan?" she asked uncertainly.

"Excellent," Claire said, although

she, too, was surprised at how quickly everything was changing already, even though it was still the same.

■ ▪ ■

After they'd sprinkled the herring in the pool, the girls waited behind the diving board. Jellyfish floated on the surface of the water, and a few bubbles arose up from the deep, but there was no sign of the mermaid. Hours passed and the girls didn't move. Time was so slow, and the air was so hot, they almost fell asleep.

When they didn't show up at the snack bar for lunch, Raymond came looking for them.

"What happened to my only customers?" he asked. "I was worried. I thought the seagulls had carried you away."

Raymond sat on the edge of a lounge chair and gazed into the pool. He was so handsome that for a few minutes the girls forgot there was a mermaid nearby.

"What a disaster," Raymond said, looking around the beach club. "I should have taken a different job this summer, but I guess I got used to this place."

When he'd first come to the Capri, he'd been the assistant to the assistant cook at the snack bar, and at lunch time they'd all had to work like crazy just to fill the orders of hamburgers and sandwiches and fries. There were crowds of people and the air smelled like coconut-scented sunscreen. Not a single one of the chaise lounges would have been empty on a beautiful day such as this. But that was all in the past.

"I don't want it to end," Raymond admitted.

"We know," the girls said at the very same time. "Neither do we."

"Don't forget to come by and have a

lemonade. My treat," Raymond said as he started back to the snack bar. "After all, there are only a few days left to the summer."

Hailey had always noticed that Raymond often read two books at a time, and Claire had always noticed that he was so kindhearted, he fed day-old bread to the seagulls that followed him as though he were their favorite person on earth. Now they both could tell he was almost as sad as they were about the Capri closing.

The girls had been watching Raymond so intently, it was a while before

they realized that a mermaid had surfaced at the shallow end of the pool.
Her hair was pale and silvery and her
nails were a shimmering blue. Between
each finger there was a thin webbing,
of the sort you might find on a new-
born seal or a duck.

"What are you two staring at?" the
mermaid said, when she turned and
saw the girls gaping.

Her voice was as cool and fresh as
bubbles rising from the ocean. She was
as beautiful as a pearl, with a faint
turquoise tinge to her skin and eyes so
blue they were the exact same color as

the deepest sea. But her watery beauty didn't mean the mermaid knew her manners.

"Stop looking at me," she demanded, as she splashed at the girls. "Go away!"

The mermaid's name was Aquamarine and she was much ruder than most creatures you might find at sea. At sixteen, she was the youngest of seven sisters, and had always been spoiled. She'd been indulged and cared for and allowed to act up in ways no self-respecting mermaid ever would.

Her disagreeable temperament certainly hadn't improved after spending two nights in the pool, tossed there like a stone or a sea urchin at the height of the terrible storm. Chlorine had seeped into her sensitive skin and silver scales dropped from her long, graceful tail. She hadn't eaten anything more than a mouthful of that horrible herring the girls had strewn into the pool.

"You heard me," Aquamarine said to Hailey and Claire, who were mesmerized by her gleaming tail and by the way the mermaid could dive so quickly, she disappeared in a luminous flash. When she surfaced through the seaweed she was not pleased to see they were still there. "Scram," she said. "Stop bothering me."

The mermaid glided into the deep end of the pool, the better to see Raymond at the snack bar. She had been watching him ever since she found herself stranded in the pool. His was the first human face she saw. She gazed at him with a bewildered expression, the sure sign of a mermaid in love.

"They're closing the Capri at the end of the week. The pool is going to be drained," Hailey called to Aquamarine. "You're going to have to go back to where you came from by Saturday."

The mermaid started to pay attention. "Where will the people go?"

"What people?" Hailey said. "Everyone's already gone except for us."

"Not exactly." Claire nodded toward Raymond. "Not everyone."

"He's going on Saturday, too," Hailey said. "He's leaving for college."

As soon as Aquamarine heard this, she began to cry blue, freshwater tears. No mermaid wants to fall in love with a human, but it was already too late for poor Aquamarine to be sensible. A sensible mermaid never would have wandered away from her sisters during a storm the way Aquamarine had.

As for Hailey and Claire, they couldn't know that a mermaid in love is far more irrational than a jellyfish and more stubborn than a barnacle. "You'll just have to go back to the ocean," they advised her.

"I'm not going anywhere."

Aquamarine's pale complexion flushed blue as she pouted. "I won't leave before I meet him."

Up at the snack bar, Raymond was whistling a tune as he cleaned up the counter. Aquamarine tilted her head to listen, hearkening to what she clearly believed was the most beautiful melody anyone had ever been privileged to hear, either on land or at sea.

"Oh," she sighed as she watched Raymond. Her elbows rested on the edge of the pool. Her sea-blue eyes were dreamy. "If he only knew how I felt about him."

"I really don't think he's your type," Claire said as politely as she could.

Aquamarine looked stricken. She had never been denied anything she wanted. "Of course he is," she said.

"Well, for one thing, he lives on land," Hailey reminded the mermaid.

"You are both so mean," Aquamarine cried. "You're meaner than my sisters, and probably just as jealous."

Since she'd been swept up by the storm and set down at the Capri, Aquamarine had felt a taste of freedom. More important than the terrible food and the chlorinated pool was the idea that she could do whatever she pleased. She tossed her head and fixed the girls with her sea-blue eyes. "No one can tell me what to do anymore. Not my sisters and certainly not you. Anyway, it's too late. I've already made up my mind. I'm staying right here for as long as I want to. And no one can tell me otherwise!"

■ ■ ■

At the end of the day, the girls ran to Claire's grandfather's car and when he said "What's new, Susie Q's?" they let out a gale of giggles, convinced that no one would believe that they'd stumbled upon a mermaid who refused to behave. When they got to Claire's grandparents' house, they raced past the half-packed boxes in the living room and looked through the crates of books in

Claire's room, hoping to find a solution for Aquamarine's predicament. Although they discovered references to many unusual creatures of the deep, from dolphins that were said to rescue lost sailors to sea-serpents twice the size of a whale, they couldn't unearth a single bit of advice on what to do with a mermaid who'd fallen in love.

That night, the girls had dinner at Hailey's house. Through the kitchen window they could see the new people, the ones who'd bought Claire's grandparents' house. They were getting a final tour of the yard to ensure that once they moved in they would know how to best care for the garden. They'd be aware of which plants would bloom to be day lilies and which ones would forever remain weeds. A red-haired girl of twelve trailed after the new people. She looked uncertain and lonely and she stopped to smell the roses that Claire's grandmother had planted beside the back door.

"Maybe she'll be your new best friend," Claire said.

"I'm never even going to talk to her," Hailey assured Claire.

"Never?" Claire said hopefully.

"Not unless there's a fire and I have to shout for her to get out of the house."

That night Claire was thinking about what might happen if there ever really was a fire; how Hailey would run over in her nightgown and pound her fists on the door to wake everyone and save them, and how the red-haired girl would always be grateful, and how no one would even remember that Claire had ever lived in that same house. Claire was so wrapped up in trying to forecast the future, that she wasn't her usual problem-solving self. Frankly, she wasn't herself at all. She nearly jumped out of her chair when the phone rang. It was the friends' special signal: one ring, then hang up, then call right back again.

Claire went into the kitchen to answer the phone. She looked through the window and across the yard to where Hailey was, in her own kitchen. All night, Claire had been wondering who she would be without Hailey to take up her plans and turn them into actions. In case of a fire, would Claire be courageous enough to knock on the door of a burning house?

Hailey waved across the yard. "I

found an encyclopedia of mythical creatures." Hailey held a red book up to the window for Claire to see.

"She's not mythological," Claire reminded her friend.

"Well, whatever she is, this book says that no mermaid can remain on land. The longest survival on record was one week in a circus and on the seventh day that mermaid dried up from head to tail. Nothing was left but a pile of green dust."

"What can we do?" Claire said. "She won't listen to us."

Unless Hailey was mistaken, Claire was actually asking for advice. Now that the responsibility rested with her, there was really no choice but for Hailey to come up with a plan, and that's exactly what she did.

"All we need to do is get her what she wants," Hailey decided. "Then she'll have to listen."

3

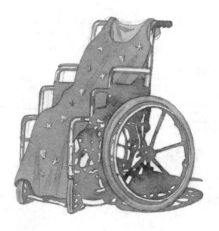

Raymond was packing his books when they found him. He had worked at the Capri for four summers, and although he still hadn't figured out how to cook a hamburger without burning the meat, he'd read one hundred and twenty-two books during his time at the beach. All the same, he wasn't sure he'd read quite enough to go to college. The future seemed like a cloud that day, the black, stormy kind it was impossible to see through, the sort that could make a person believe that blue skies would never again return.

But Raymond's worrying was interrupted when the girls ran to the snack counter to tell him they needed his help. They had a cousin visiting, they told him, from overseas, which wasn't so far from the truth. To make certain their cousin wouldn't be bored, the girls wanted Raymond to have dinner with her the following night.

"How can you have the same cousin?" Raymond was confused. "I didn't even think you were related."

"It's through marriage," Hailey said because she'd heard other people use that excuse to explain complicated family relationships.

"And divorce," Claire added, because she'd heard that as well.

"Anyway, she's a very distant cousin," Hailey said. "We just want her to have a good time while she's here. All you have to do is show up in the cafeteria at six o'clock tomorrow night."

■   ■   ■

After Raymond had agreed to the dinner, Claire began to wonder how Hailey kept coming up with all these ideas, one after another, as if they just popped into her head. Now, for instance, Hailey raced to the pool, where she sat with her feet dangling in the shallow end. She took a can of tuna and an opener from her backpack, having remembered that the mermaid would be hungry.

"Good thinking," Claire said to her friend.

Claire sat beside Hailey, but was careful not to hang her feet over the edge of the pool. She looked into the water, and gingerly dipped one toe in. It wasn't quite as cold as they'd thought it might be. Just to be safe, she held on to the concrete.

■　■　■

When they told Aquamarine of her date with Raymond, she let out a shriek of joy that chased the perching seagulls into the sky.

"You only have to promise one thing," the girls reminded her. "After tomorrow, you'll go."

Aquamarine begged and cried until the pool was awash with blue tears which stained the moon jellyfish turquoise and indigo, but the girls would not change their minds.

"We're doing this for your own good," they said. "We want what's best for you."

Without saltwater, they told her, Aquamarine's skin would soon dry up until her fresh face became grainy as sand, her beautiful pale hair would curl like seaweed, her tail would turn limp and dull. Already, her time away from the ocean had caused her to fade, so that when she blushed or was angry she turned silver rather than blue. The webbing between her fingers had fallen away, and her hands looked like those of any ordinary girl. Out in the waves, her six sisters were calling for her. They missed her and worried and at high tide they came dangerously close to shore in their search.

"All right," Aquamarine said finally. "I promise I'll go."

Upon making this vow, the mermaid cried even harder.

"Cheer up," Claire said. "You'll

always remember the night you had together."

But now that Aquamarine was to get her heart's desire, she was nervous. "What if he doesn't like me?" she wondered.

Although at first Aquamarine had been happy enough to be free of her sisters, the truth was she'd been coddled and protected for so long that she couldn't seem to figure anything out on her own. She had never even braided her long, silver hair, for there had always been her sisters' twelve hands to turn the strands into plaits.

"I look dreadful," the mermaid

said. Indeed, her hair was stringy and her fingertips were puckered and pale. "I don't even have anything to wear."

"Claire can solve that problem," Hailey said.

"I can?" Claire really hadn't a clue as to what she could do to help out. How could she think straight? Her whole life was packed up and sitting in her grandparents' garage. When the moving van came to cart everything away, she wasn't sure she'd even know who she was anymore.

"I'll get one of my mother's dresses," Hailey said, "and you can make it beautiful, the way you always do."

Although Claire was pleased by the compliment, she was thoughtful as well. "One problem," she whispered. "What do we do about the tail?"

"Oh, the tail."

The girls studied Aquamarine solemnly, staring until she covered her face with her hands.

"I'm horrid," the mermaid despaired. "I'd be better off falling in love with a dolphin or a shark. It's no use. It's hopeless. I might as well stay in this pool until they drain it and take me away."

At that, Aquamarine sunk to the depths of the murky water. All the girls could see of her were little bubbles rising and popping as they hit the air.

"She's probably right." Claire crouched down to peer into the deep end. She splashed her hands in the cold salty water, hoping to call Aquamarine to the surface, but there was no response. Not a flicker, not a fin, not a face. "It *is* hopeless. How could we ever hide her tail?"

"I've got it!" Hailey said. She couldn't have been more pleased with herself, not even if she'd managed a perfect swan dive. "We'll say she's had an accident. She can't walk, just like your grandfather last winter."

That afternoon they ran to Claire's grandfather's car in the parking lot, threw themselves inside, and begged to borrow Maury's wheelchair before he could begin to get out the words *Susie Q's*.

"Please," the girls cried. "It's for a friend, and you don't need it anymore."

When they got home, Claire's grandfather unearthed the wheelchair from the bottom of a pile of odds and ends set out for the moving men. Hailey's mother found a blue dress at the back of her closet that she had worn to a dance years ago, before Hailey had even been born.

Later that night, after the grown-ups had gone to sleep, Claire went to her room and opened the last box she had packed. This was where she kept all the treasures of summers past. There were angel wings and creamy oyster shells, tiny starfish and pink rocks. She stitched every one onto the blue dress, so that the fabric shone in the moonlight, sighing as though it had just been fished out of the sea. Claire had decided not to think about the fact that in twenty-four hours she would have to set off for Florida. She wasn't going to think about what it would be like when there was no one next door to make secret phone calls to late at night, and no one to wave at through the open kitchen windows.

"It's perfect," Hailey declared over the phone when Claire held the dress up to the window for her to see. The blue fabric moved in the breeze. "He'll fall in love with her the minute he sees her."

Both girls were so sure of this they wouldn't have been the least surprised to discover that all night long Raymond dreamed of high tides and deep blue seas, and that at the bottom of the Capri's pool, where the moon jellyfish glittered like stars, Aquamarine braided her long, silvery hair and tried her best to ignore her sisters' song, which reached up from the ocean to call her home.

4

THEY DECIDED TO TELL Claire's grandfather. For one thing, he wasn't like most grown-ups — he actually listened to what they had to say — and for another, the girls needed to stay at the Capri until nine, in order to take

Aquamarine home from her date with Raymond. After they had recounted the story of the mermaid in love, Maury didn't say a word. He didn't say he'd never heard such nonsense before. He didn't say, *Maloney baloney,* which he sometimes shouted out when he didn't believe some bit of news he heard on the radio. The way he listened made Claire realize how fortunate she was to have him as her grandfather. He even drove them to the beach that morning, telling Hailey's mom he wanted to chauffeur the girls as a way to say good-bye, since the next day was

Saturday, their last day at the club. Although this excuse was true enough, the other reason he drove wasn't mentioned: The wheelchair fit neatly into the trunk of his car.

"I know you won't believe this," Maury said when they got to the beach, "but you're not the only ones who've ever seen a mermaid. I've spotted several myself down in Florida, although I admit I've never gotten to know one personally. When you think about it, you are two lucky girls."

Maury told them to have a good time and not to worry. He'd be waiting in the parking lot at nine and, like most people who've seen mermaids, even from a distance, he could be depended on not to tell.

Hailey and Claire borrowed a hammer they found in one of the abandoned cabanas to open the boarded-up cafeteria. Once inside, they swept the layer of sand from the floor and dusted the cobwebs off tables and chairs. After that was accomplished, they set out the dinner Hailey had thought to bring along, a carefully planned menu of tuna-fish sandwiches, seaweed salad, and sardines on toast. There was spring water for Raymond and a glass of saltwater, perfectly chilled for Aquamarine.

When they got to the pool, they saw that the water had turned so murky that the shallow end resembled a tidal pool. Purple snails climbed the metal rungs of the stairs and seagulls dived to scoop up the little silver fish that swam past the mosaic tiles. Aquamarine was waiting for them. She was even more faded than she'd been the day before, her tail withering to white, her complexion turning chalky, but when she saw the dress they held up, she turned blue with delight.

"Come and get me out," the mermaid

demanded, and then she thought better of what she had said. "Please," she amended. "Help me."

"How do we get her out?" Claire asked Hailey.

"We have to go into the pool and carry her," Hailey said. "There is no other way."

Claire turned cold at the very thought. "But I don't swim," she reminded her friend.

"You don't have to," Hailey assured her. "All you have to do is wade into the shallow end."

And so they went into the pool slowly, and only as deep as their waists.

But even in three feet of water, Claire was fearful, especially when the moon jellies floated near. Still, the girls managed to carry Aquamarine out, and they lifted her onto the wheelchair. After that, they helped her get dressed in one of the abandoned cabanas. When they cleaned off the mirror and Aquamarine finally saw her reflection, she made a sound that was somewhere between laughter and a wave breaking.

"Oh, thank you," she said, completely delighted. "I look like a real girl."

As they wheeled Aquamarine to the cafeteria, the sun began to set. Thankfully, the air was turning cooler — still being on land had begun to affect the mermaid. Out of saltwater, she was rapidly drying up. Claire had to collect the trail of scales that were shedding from her silvery tail.

"What if he doesn't like me?" Aquamarine worried. "What if I'm all wrong?"

But she had nothing to worry about. Hailey and Claire knew that for certain because the moment Raymond saw her, he looked as though he were drowning.

"She's your cousin?" he said to the girls. "I've never seen anyone like her before."

"That's because she isn't like anyone else. She's special," Hailey told Raymond.

"And she's had an accident, sort of, so don't ask her to dance."

Hailey and Claire waited outside on the patio. They pulled up lounge chairs and listened to the murmur of voices and the beautiful sound of Aquamarine's watery laughter. Up in the summer sky, there were so many stars a person would never be able to count them all. Claire wondered if there would be the exact same stars in Florida, and if when she gazed out her window she'd still be looking at the same constellations that Hailey saw.

"That new girl with the red hair isn't so horrible," Claire said. "Her name is Susanna. Susie Q. You get it?" The new people had come back again, and Claire had showed Susanna the room that would soon be hers. "She's actually nice."

"I don't care," Hailey said. "It doesn't really matter to me if she's nice or not. I'm never talking to her."

"Unless there's a fire," Claire reminded her friend.

"Or an earthquake," Hailey said grudgingly.

"You'd have to," Claire said. "You'd have no choice."

"But I'd never call her on the phone with our code."

"No. You never would."

Sometimes it was a comfort to say the thing you were most afraid of aloud. Tonight, Claire felt certain that stars would shine as brightly, no matter where a person was when she watched them. Even if someone was at the bottom of the deepest sea, the light would find her.

■ ▢ ■

When it was nearly nine o'clock, the girls went to retrieve Aquamarine. Silvery moonlight was spilling into the cafeteria. Raymond looked a little stunned when the girls said he'd better say good-bye to their cousin. Time had a habit of moving too fast. Anyone could see that from the expression on Raymond's face.

"Already?" he said mournfully. All last night he had dreamed of the ocean, and now it seemed to him that he might be dreaming still.

"It's not time," Aquamarine insisted. "It can't be over."

But it was. Beneath the wheelchair a circle of fish scales the color of moonlight had collected. Each one was now evaporating into fine, green dust.

"Can I have your phone number?" Raymond asked the mermaid as the girls hurried to wheel her out the door. "Your address?"

"No," Hailey and Claire said at the same time. "She's going away."

"I'm going away, too," Raymond said, confused.

"Well, she's going farther," Claire told him.

"She's going someplace you can't ever get to," Hailey added.

But Aquamarine knew better. She unhooked one of the shells from her beautiful blue dress and gave it to Raymond. She promised that if he said her name into the shell, she would hear him, no matter where she might be.

"I don't think that's possible." Raymond shook his head. He'd read so many books that he thought he knew how every story ended.

"Anything is possible," Aquamarine told him, and when the girls looked at her face, they knew that this was true.

Aquamarine didn't say a word when the girls brought her back to the pool. If she was crying, she didn't let them see. Tomorrow at noon, high tide would race in. Aquamarine was sure of this because a mermaid can always tell the tide, just as easily as a person can distinguish night from day. It was then she'd have to leave.

The girls stored the wheelchair in an abandoned cabana and promised they'd be back in the morning, first thing. Aquamarine had become so weak from her stay on land she hadn't any strength left. She was too exhausted to swim and was forced to stay in the shallow end of the pool. All the same, she refused to take off the blue dress, even though it weighed her down. By now, Aquamarine was as pale as those fish you find beached on the shore, and she'd begun to labor for breath.

"This is the most beautiful night there has ever been," the mermaid whispered.

The girls ran to the parking lot where Maury was dozing behind the wheel of his car.

"So," he asked when they got in the car. "Was your mermaid happy with tonight's results?"

"She said it was the most beautiful night there had ever been," Claire said.

When the girls looked around them, they saw that this was true. Hailey and Claire peered back through the Capri gates, to the beach where the white crests of the waves broke on the shore. They could see the stars sparkling above. To have a night like this could make almost anyone believe in the future.

■　■　■

The furniture in Claire's grandparents' house was gone now, and because of this they were all supposed to sleep at Hailey's. But the girls begged and pleaded and at last the grown-ups gave in and allowed them to take their sleeping bags and camp out in the empty living room at Claire's house. It felt funny to be there without the sofa and the table and the pillows and the books and everything else that had made this Claire's home. Their voices echoed off the bare walls.

"Do you think she'll really go tomorrow?" Hailey asked.

"She has to," Claire said. "She doesn't have a choice."

"Well, I wish she could stay." Hailey's voice sounded strange, as though she were about to cry, but of course it was Claire who had always been the crier, not Hailey. Or at least this had been true up until now.

"You know what?" Right then Claire felt certain that some things really did stay the same. "I think she wishes that, too."

5

On Saturday, the owner of the Capri Beach Club returned, along with his wife, his children, his grandchildren, all his uncles and aunts, and everyone who had ever worked at the Capri. A good-bye party was being held, with

live music and a barbecue and more
people than the beach club had seen
all summer long. The line at the snack
bar crisscrossed the patio, with crowds
calling for sandwiches and sodas.

Streamers and balloons had been
strung over the entranceway. Even the
bulldozers had been decorated. But de-
spite the crepe paper necklaces and the
headdresses of streamers, the machines
looked like yellow monsters. No one
could disguise that their purpose was
to dismantle the club.

"Where have all these people been
all summer?" Hailey grumbled when
she and Claire arrived. The girls made

their way through the crowd. "The one day we want some privacy, this place is mobbed."

They spied Raymond, who had already packed up his books and was leaving for Florida later that day. He was working hard, trying to keep up with the demand of the crowd, but when he noticed the girls, he left everything and came over. He had the white shell Aquamarine had given him on a chain around his neck. He looked as though he hadn't had a wink of sleep.

"How can I leave without saying good-bye to her?" he said to the girls.

"You'll just have to," Hailey said.

"We all have to do what we don't want to do sometimes," Claire added.

The girls looked nervously at the pool. At least the warning ropes were still up and none of the crowd had yet ventured near.

"Is there something you're not telling me?" Raymond asked.

One little boy was approaching the deep end. He had a fishing net in his hands and a look on his face that spelled trouble.

"Fishy," the little boy said.

"If there's something we're not telling you, we're not telling you for your own good," Claire said. "And for Aquamarine's good, too."

The little boy was standing at the very edge of the pool, teetering on the cement.

"Oh, no!" Hailey said.

"Get back here!" Claire cried.

But the little boy didn't listen, and as they watched, he fell with barely a splash into the murky water. When Raymond saw what had happened, he ran so fast the girls could hardly keep up. He dove into the pool with his clothes and his shoes on. The girls could hear the little boy's parents calling to find their dear Arthur who was always such a wanderer.

His parents had no idea that Arthur

had already been saved, and was secure in Raymond's and Aquamarine's arms. Someone else might have been shocked to see the silvery tail which guided Aquamarine through the water, but if anything, Raymond's eyes shone even brighter when he looked at her. As for the mermaid, she had used her last bit of strength to catch the boy when he fell. She was now as pale as moonlight, and so weak Raymond had to help her back to the shallow end of the pool. Thankfully, Arthur was so surprised to find that the fish he'd discovered was a girl that he didn't say a word.

"We have to take her back now," Hailey said. "We can't wait another minute!"

Raymond and Aquamarine looked at each other. Neither one wanted the other to leave, but without the ocean Aquamarine would fade into dust. By now, everyone was searching for Arthur and the crowd was coming dangerously close.

"Go on," Raymond told the girls. "I'll take care of things here."

Aquamarine turned to him then. Her voice was light as sea mist. "Wherever you are," she said. "I'll find you."

While the girls carried Aquamarine

out of the pool to place her in the wheelchair she whispered something that sounded like *thank you.* She had become so dehydrated from her time on land that she was now surprisingly light and all that was left of her voice was a trickle.

Raymond went to the far end of the pool and waved his arms in the air. "Over here," he called to the crowd. He had wrapped Arthur in a blanket and now he lifted the boy up for all to see. Everyone turned to look, and in that moment the girls slipped away with Aquamarine.

The crowd surged around the rescued Arthur. People cheered and called Raymond a hero, and not one of them noticed that Raymond was paying no attention to their acclaim. He was looking to make sure the girls were on their way to the sea, wishing only that Aquamarine would be safe.

Hailey and Claire were already racing the wheelchair past the tennis courts where the weeds were as tall as trees, past the cabanas that hadn't been used all summer long, past the snack bar where Raymond would never work again. The owner of the beach club spied them, and he yelled for them to stay off the beach, but they went on anyway, past the bulldozers, until the sand was too deep to roll the wheelchair along. They had reached the seawall, made of cement and stones, which stood four feet tall.

"We have to carry her over," Hailey said.

By now, the mermaid was light as air, dusty and dry as the sand. The girls made a seat for her out of their crossed arms and Aquamarine held onto their shoulders. Together, they made their way over the cement wall, then jumped down into the water. It was high tide and the surf was rough, but it was the time when the mermaid had to go. They could hear the owner yelling at them, but his words were lost in the crashing noise at the shore.

"We're going to have to bring her all the way in, past the breaking waves," Claire said.

Hailey looked at her friend who had always been so afraid of water and felt immensely proud of her.

Together they carried Aquamarine. Her long hair blew out behind her and her skin gave off puffs of greenish dust, as if she were already turning to ash, right there in their arms.

"Hurry," Claire shouted over the sound of the surf. "We're losing her."

They went in past the whitecaps that shone like stars, past the water that was wilder than horses. Over the crashing they could hear the sound of the mermaid's six sisters singing to her, urging her to quickly return to where she belonged.

Aquamarine seemed too weak to swim. At first, she was so limp she could not lift her head, but the farther into the water they brought her, the more she revived. Soon she splashed her tail, and before long she began to shimmer again, and when she laughed her watery laugh, they could tell it was time to let go. By then, the girls were up to their necks in the surf, doing their best to stay afloat in the rolling waves.

"We'll never forget you," the girls told her, and at the very same moment, they opened their arms. Before they could blink, she was gone, deep into the waves, to the very bottom of the sea where her sisters were waiting to rejoice and take her home and keep her safe all the rest of her days.

By the time the girls helped each other back to shore, their arms and legs were aching, but they didn't want to let go of one another. They had both swallowed quarts of saltwater. They pulled strands of seaweed from their hair as they watched the sea, but all they could see were the waves. Aquamarine had disappeared without a trace. The girls might have felt as though they'd imagined her completely if they hadn't found the two white shells Aquamarine had left for them on the seat of the wheelchair. They were beautiful shells, as white as the surf in the sea. When you held one up to your ear you could hear the sound of your best friend talking to you, even if she was a thousand miles away.

"What did I tell you girls!" the owner of the Capri shouted when Hailey and Claire waved to Raymond as he headed for the parking lot and roared off on his motorbike. "Stay off the beach!"

"We just wanted to say good-bye," they told him. And then they hugged the startled owner and thanked him for the best summer of their lives.

■　■　■

That evening, while dusk was spreading across the sky, Claire's grandparents loaded up their car. The moving men had taken most of their belongings, but Claire had set aside anything that was irreplaceable. These items would be taken along on the ride down to Florida, to ensure they wouldn't get lost. There was the pearl necklace that had belonged to Claire's mother, and the photograph albums, and one of the white shells left by Aquamarine.

Hailey's mom had made up a picnic basket, with deviled eggs and chocolate cupcakes and a Thermos of pink lemonade, and she'd thrown in the necessities for anyone who leaves home: a compass, a map, and a photograph of the house that was left behind.

"It's all right if you talk to the girl who moves in here," Claire told Hailey as her grandparents were buckling their seat belts and waving good-bye. "I've thought it over, and I really want you to."

"I might say hello or something. Just to be polite."

"Even if there isn't a fire," they both said at the very same time, the way they were still known to do.

Hailey and Claire hugged each other right there on the lawn that Claire's grandfather had cared for so meticulously. It was still the best lawn in the neighborhood, and Hailey would be around to make certain the new people watered early in the morning, which was always best for any garden.

Hailey stood where she was and waved until Claire's grandparents' car disappeared. After that, she stood there a while longer. It was still August, but it didn't feel like summer anymore. All of a sudden the crickets' call was faster, as if they knew that in only a week school would begin. It was obvious, even to the insects, that it would be quite some time before the weather turned hot again.

That night, Hailey's mom fixed rainbow sundaes, which had always been Claire and Hailey's favorite treat. Vanilla ice cream, strawberries, blueberries, hot fudge, and butterscotch. But Hailey couldn't eat. She went to the kitchen window even though it wasn't possible to see anything next door. Just an empty house, without any curtains, or any people, or anything at all. Hailey got out her white seashell and she held it to her ear. The whooshing sound within was exactly like Claire's voice, and Hailey hoped that if she spoke into the shell Claire would hear her, no matter how far away she already was. *Safe trip,* that's what she called to her friend. *Here's to the future,* she said.

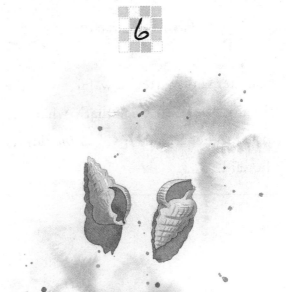

ON THE DAY THE BULLDOZERS
knocked down the Capri Beach Club,
the weather changed at last. The sky
was as gray as fish scales and the air
was salty and wet. Hailey and her

mom stood in the parking lot to watch. Before long, the entranceway was crushed, the patio was leveled, and the fence around the pool was shoved aside. Hundreds of seagulls and terns circled in the sky.

The pool had already been drained, and in no time the bulldozers set to work breaking down the concrete. It was hard to tell which was noisier, the sound of the machines at work or the rumble of the wild surf.

Hailey had brought her camera along, and she'd planned to take a photograph to send to Claire so that she could see what had happened to the Capri, but it didn't even seem like the same place anymore.

"I think it's better if she just remembers it the way it was," Hailey told her mother.

True enough, some things were best kept as a memory, but some things changed for the better. Claire, for instance, had taken up swimming, which only made sense since she now lived right on the beach. As it turned out, she was good at it. She took to the water if not like a mermaid, then at least like a fish.

Of course, if she hadn't started

swimming, she would have never run into Raymond, who was on his college team and often practiced in the blue bay that Claire could see from her window. The first time she spotted him, Claire thought Raymond was a seal, that's how far out in the water he was, but then he waved to her and swam over.

"I never thanked you and your friend for introducing me to Aquamarine," Raymond said.

"I'm sorry it didn't work out," Claire said.

"But it did." Raymond was surprised. "She said she would find me, and she did."

When he swam back into the sea, Claire could see that he wasn't really alone. There in the deepest blue water was a girl who was waiting for him, far beyond the breaking waves. For some time afterward, Claire brought her camera down to the beach, hoping for a photograph of Aquamarine to send to Hailey. But after a while she put her camera away. Hailey would be coming to visit next summer and that wasn't so very far away. If they were lucky, if they watched carefully, they might still be able to spy Aquamarine. Far beyond the tide pools and the jellyfish, beyond starfish and snails, she is swimming there still.

AFTer WorDS™

Alice Hoffman's

Aquamarine

Contents

After Words™ guide by Anica Mrose Rissi

About the Author

Alice Hoffman was born in New York City and raised in a working-class neighborhood on Long Island. As a child, Alice adored fairy tales, from the Brothers Grimm to the folk stories she heard from her Russian grandmother. Many of the books Alice has written as an adult contain doses of fairy-tale magic. She is known for writing stories that weave the wondrous and unexpected with the commonplace.

Alice wrote her first novel, *Property Of*, at age twenty-one, while she was working toward her MFA in creative writing at Stanford University. Since then, she has published more than fifteen novels for adults and two books of short fiction. Her six books for children include the novels *Aquamarine*, *Indigo*, and *Green Angel* and the picture book *Moondog*, which she wrote with her son Wolfe Martin. Alice has also written many screenplays with her husband, Tom Martin. Her work has been published around the world and translated into more than twenty languages.

Alice, her husband, and their dogs live in an old Victorian house near Boston. She is the mother of two sons.

Q&A with Alice Hoffman

Q: Aquamarine *is being turned into a movie (as was your adult novel* Practical Magic*). What is the book-to-movie process like? Were you involved with the script? Did you visit the set? What is it like to see the characters you brought to life on the page appear on the screen?*

A: I didn't visit the set because it was in Australia (!!!) and I live in Boston. But I was sent e-mail photos all through the shoot, and saw how the crew built an entire beach club on the beach! I also heard that all the girls in the movie were given swimming lessons and that one day they were surrounded by dolphins during their lessons, which we all felt was good luck. It's always fun to see characters become "real people," and interesting to see how an actor interprets a character.

Q: *You write screenplays as well as novels. When you write your novels, do you imagine them as films? Do movies influence your books in other ways?*

A: Novels and screenplays are very different to write. Screenplays have a format — they're 120 pages, for instance — and are set in acts like a play. A novel can be anything you want it to be. With screenplays, a writer works with lots of other people, and writing a novel can be lonely. But, of course, the writer is in charge of everything!!!

Q: *Several of your books take place near water or contain water imagery. What is your connection to the water?*
A: I grew up near the water and spent summers at a beach club very much like the one in *Aquamarine*. I'm also a Pisces — and that's the water sign. I can't imagine living very far from the ocean.

Q: Aquamarine, Indigo, Green Angel . . . *many of your book titles contain colors. Any reason for this? Do colors color your own life as much as they do your characters'?*
A: Color finds its way into my work — color is very evocative when it comes to feelings and emotions. I used to paint my office a different color every time I started a book, but now I'm tired of that, so I painted it brown!

Q: *Is it true that when you were growing up, you wanted to be a hairdresser? How did you end up becoming a writer instead?*
A: I didn't know what I wanted to be when I grew

up. I was a big reader and always had a book with me, but I didn't think it was possible for me to become a writer. It just goes to show — follow your dream.

Q: *Any advice for aspiring writers?*
A: The best advice I can give to young writers is to write!!! The more you write, the better you become. And to read. The more you read, the more you experience the many different literary possibilities open to you.

Q: *You have written a lot of books. Does writing novels get easier the more often you do it?*
A: Writing is always hard. The first part is creative and fun, but for me the rewrites are a lot like writing a term paper. All writers rewrite and work hard, but it's worth the time and effort.

Q: *What is your writing routine like?*
A: I write every day. For me it's a lot more fulfilling than reading at this point, because I'm inventing the story.

Q: *What do you do when you aren't writing?*
A: When I'm not writing, I spend a lot of time with

my three dogs, Cody, Angel, and Skylar. I LOVE to go to the beach and walk.

Q: *What inspired you to write* Aquamarine?
A: I had a best friend who moved away, which spurred the idea of the book. We went to a beach club one summer on Long Island, where I grew up. I have spent most of my summers at the beach, even when I lived in northern California and the water was too cold for swimming!

Q: *The Capri Beach Club is such a vivid and important part of the story — it almost feels like a character in the book. Did the setting come to you fully formed, or was it built one piece at a time? What came first — the characters or the place?*
A: With this book, the characters and the place came together. They all belonged together. And then a mermaid appeared in the pool, and there was the story.

Q: *Do you believe in mermaids?*
A: Definitely.

Raymond's Lemonade

Stir up a summer treat that's sure to please . . . whether you're near a pool or not!

Ingredients

1 cup freshly squeezed lemon juice (from 6 large lemons)

1 cup ice

⅔ cup sugar

5 cups cold water

Directions

1. Put the lemon juice and ice in a blender. Blend until slushy.
2. Pour the lemon slush into a large pitcher.
3. Add the sugar and water. Stir until the sugar dissolves.
4. Serve over ice in tall glasses with colorful straws.

Variation

Strawberry Lemonade

For an extra-special treat, add one cup of sliced strawberries to the blender with the lemon juice and ice.

Make Your Own Memory Box

Do you have a summer, a place, an experience, or a friend that you never want to forget? A memory box is the perfect place to store pieces of your past. Here are a few ideas for putting yours together.

- Start by choosing a lining for the inside of the box. Perhaps you'll paste in a few pages from a local newspaper, a photocopy of some sheet music, or a piece of paper the same color as your walls.
- Collect memory joggers to store in your box, such as a bag of sand from an oft-visited beach, pressed flowers from a grandparent's garden, or a ticket stub from a favorite movie. Use construction paper and a gel pen to create labels for the items in your box and tie them on with ribbon or string.
- Write down a few of the sounds, colors, smells, sayings, or other things you want to remember. Your box could include a playlist of the songs you listened to all summer, a description of your favorite room, or a list of words that come to mind when you think of your best friend.
- Decorate the outside of your memory box with poster paints, collage, glitter, or wrapping paper. Label it with the month, year, and place you've captured inside.

Best-friend Signals

Hailey and Claire use a special phone signal — one ring, then hang up, then call right back again — to let each other know who's calling. Here are some ideas for signals that you and your best friend can use to communicate without saying a word.

- Choose a secret knock to use on each other's front doors. Try knocking a rhythm that can be set to words — that way, it will be easier to remember and recognize. The words can be silly, like "Mississippi hot dog" (four short knocks followed by two long ones), or practical, like "Hey — it's me!" (knock, pause, knock-knock). When your best friend uses the secret knock, you'll know who's at the door before you even open it.
- When you and your best friend pass notes, the way you fold the paper can send a message about its contents. Is the note extra-extra top secret? Let your BF know that right away by folding the note into a triangle. Is the note urgent — must be read right away? Fold it into a fan. If you want your friend to write back, fold the note into a square. If she should destroy the note after she has read it, crumple the paper into a ball before you pass it to her.

- Need to communicate something important to your best friend while other people are around? No problem — use your own "private eye" code.

Blink twice: *Let's get out of here.*
Left eye wink: *He's cute!*
Right eye wink: *You've got something stuck in your teeth.*
Rapid blink with eyebrows raised: *I really need to talk to you — alone.*
Eyebrow wiggle: *I'm so glad we're here together!*

A Sneak Peek at *Indigo*

A haunted town. A watery journey.
Two unusual brothers.
Don't miss Alice Hoffman's *Indigo*.

The town of Oak Grove was so far away from the ocean that most people who lived there had never seen a seagull or listened to the whisper of a pink shell. They certainly hadn't heard the way the sea can call to you on a hot July day when wave after wave beckons and the water is endless and clear.

As a matter of fact, people in Oak Grove dreaded water. This was a town with a history of terrible flooding. Fifteen years earlier, the spring that fed Penman's Creek overflowed, leaving Oak Grove awash so that people had to clamor onto their roofs. When the flood-waters finally receded, the creek was dammed up, and folks went overboard to protect Oak Grove. The town council ordered the public swimming pool drained; lawn watering was limited to an hour a day, showers to ten minutes long. Drier was better in Oak Grove, or so people said. And the weather appeared to cooperate. The only thing that seemed endless here was the perfect blue sky that was the same day after day, without the slightest hint of rain or the hope of a stray cloud passing by.

Most residents of Oak Grove were grateful for its climate. But not Martha Glimmer.

As far as Martha was concerned, this was the worst year of her life. Martha hated Oak

Grove, where there was nothing better to do on a brilliant spring day than sit on the roof of her father's garage with her two best friends, Trevor and Eli McGill, and throw rocks at the line of tin cans they'd arranged down below.

Martha hated the fact that it never rained in Oak Grove; she hated the way the grass grew so dry, it creaked when you walked on it; and she hated Hildy Swoon, a neighbor who brought casseroles over almost every night and tried to convince Martha's father that he should start a new life. Most of all, Martha hated people who pitied a girl like herself, who'd lost her mother the year before, at such a tender age. While Martha was at it, she hated being thirteen, a number that was clearly unlucky, at least for her, for this was the year when she'd grown seven inches; her legs were now so long and gawky, she often tripped over her own feet.

Martha's friend, Trevor McGill, completely disagreed; he enjoyed being thirteen. He had grown taller as well, one of the few boys their age who was the same height as Martha. But whereas Martha was uncomfortable with her size, Trevor couldn't be happier with his. As for Trevor's brother, Eli, at eleven, he was at an age when anything older was preferable, and could hardly wait to grow up.

Both the McGill brothers had dark hair and sea-green eyes, and they certainly weren't like anyone else in town. It wasn't anything obvious that set the boys apart, but when you considered some of their odder traits, the little things added up. From the time the boys were toddlers there had been gossip about them. Susie Lawrence, who worked at the Sweet Shoppe, confided that the boys threw away any candy their mother bought them, tossing out jelly beans and chocolate bars alike, and that wasn't very normal, was it? Their old baby-sitter, Gretchen Hardy, whispered that Trevor and Eli had refused to nap unless she brought them into the kitchen. They'd cry and bellow like walruses until Gretchen turned on the tap full blast, and then, instantly, the sound of running water lulled them to sleep.

As the boys grew older, they grew stranger as well, or so people said, especially those folks who enjoyed gossip far more than they enjoyed their neighbors' good fortune. But who could blame people for discussing how odd it was that Eli McGill had been found splashing around in a bathtub — thankfully, with all his clothes on — at Annamaria Chamberlain's tenth birthday party while everyone else devoured cake and ice cream. Or how unnerving it was when Trevor fixed people with his pale green eyes, staring until even the most landlocked citizens found themselves dreaming of running off to sea with the wind at their backs and everything else in their lives just a memory.